Into Thin Air

Published in 2010 by Evans Publishing Ltd,
2A Portman Mansions,
Chiltern St, London WIU 6NR

Editor: Su Swallow
Designer: D.R. Ink

British Library Cataloguing in Publication Data

Harrison, Paul, 1969-
Into thin air. -- (Take 2)
1. Children's stories.
I. Title II. Series
823.9'2-dc22

ISBN-13: 9780237542054

Printed in China.

Into Thin Air

Paul Harrison and Doreen Lang

Evans

Contents

An Unusual Trip

It was Imogen's annual trip to visit her favourite aunt, Elisabeth.
Imogen had been excited for weeks, but now that she had
arrived it was something of a disappointment.

Elisabeth was a research scientist working at laboratories high in the mountains. She always let Imogen come and help with the experiments, but this time she seemed less keen.

"Well, it is a secure site after all – there aren't meant to be visitors," Elisabeth explained.

"It's never stopped me going before," Imogen replied petulantly.

"I just don't think it's a good idea at the moment."

Imogen kept pestering her while she unpacked, and eventually Elisabeth relented.

The drive to the laboratories never failed to impress Imogen. The twisting road through the mountains with their precipitous drops was truly exhilarating.

When they arrived, the laboratories were a hive of activity. Enormous meteorological balloons were being inflated with hydrogen. They would be launched into the upper levels of the atmosphere to take readings for the final parts of Elisabeth's experiments.

A Strange Atmosphere

Elisabeth took Imogen to the main control room that overlooked the launch zone. There scientists were looking at weather charts and calibrating the equipment while others were monitoring and controlling the flow of hydrogen into the balloons.

Things felt peculiar though. People usually said hello when she visited, but today she got barely a glance.

The more Imogen watched, the more she felt something wasn't right; and whenever Imogen tried to ask her aunt anything she seemed snappy. So Imogen just sat in the corner of the laboratory doodling as Elisabeth watched the balloons ascending and descending.

Eventually Elisabeth came over.

"I'm sorry," Elisabeth said, "this must be interminably boring for you. It's just…" she struggled to find the precise words. "We've had some… difficulties."

"What do you mean?" asked Imogen.

"Stuff's been going missing – research information. We don't know who it is – it's like the culprit disappears into thin air. The atmosphere's a bit tense now; we've just got the final results in and they need to be kept secret until we've processed the data."

Imogen looked concerned, but Elisabeth smiled.

The Balloon Flight

"Look, why not ask Barry Hoskins to go up in the observation blimp. His experiments are finished now, so it shouldn't be a bother."

This was great news. Imogen had dreamed of going up in the blimp, but had never had the opportunity.

The observation blimp was a tethered helium balloon that sat to one side of the launch zone. A small basket was suspended underneath with some simple controls for making the balloon go up and down.

Hoskins was loitering around next to the blimp. Although his work was finished he still looked pensive, and he clearly wasn't overjoyed when Imogen turned up.

"You want to what?" he exclaimed.

"Sorry, but my Aunt Elisabeth said it would probably be OK because you'd finished…"

"Yes, yes, alright," he replied testily, "but you'll have to go up by yourself. I've got stuff to do, despite what your aunt thinks."

He quickly showed Imogen how the controls worked and left her to get on with it.

Slowly, as Imogen wasn't quite sure of herself, she allowed the blimp to ascend. The basket creaked ominously beneath her, but Imogen had waited too long for an opportunity like this to let her fears overcome her now.

The view from the blimp was absolutely breathtaking. Using binoculars, Imogen could see the mountain range disappearing into the deep blue of the distance, while the lone road to the laboratories wound out below her like a ribbon. A flash of reflected sunlight caught her eye. A car was stopping round the bend from the main entrance.

Caught in the Act

Imogen watched as a man got out. Keeping low he edged around the outside of the wire-mesh fence. Eventually he broke cover, scampering over to where someone was waiting for him behind the fence. Annoyingly Imogen couldn't see who it was the man was talking to as he had his back to her.

Imogen adjusted the magnification – just in time to see the stranger pass a package through the mesh. The stranger then scurried off and the other man turned back towards the laboratories. It was then that Imogen saw who it was – Hoskins!

She had to tell her aunt!

Imogen got the blimp to descend as quickly as she could and sprinted for the control room. All of the staff were there celebrating the end of their experiments; all except Hoskins.

"Aunt Elisabeth, Aunt Elisabeth!" she cried breathlessly. "I know who the thief is, it's…"

The door to the control room slammed shut. Imogen span around to see Hoskins's self-satisfied face smiling through the small window in the door. He jangled a set of keys at them, and then disappeared.

Elisabeth dashed to the door – it was locked!

"Quick, ring the police," said one of the scientists.

"I'm on it," replied another.

"I'm sure he's got a getaway car waiting," said Elisabeth with a resigned sigh. "He'll be long gone before anyone will get here."

"But I don't understand," said Imogen. "Why's he done it?"

"Those results are bound to be valuable to some company or other," Elisabeth replied. "He's probably negotiated a good price for himself. It'll certainly pay better than research work."

From the window, they watched Hoskins stop to make a call on his mobile. And that was when Imogen had a brain wave. She noticed that he had stopped in a loop of cable attached to one of the meteorological balloons.

"Quick," Imogen said, pointing to the cable, "the hydrogen."

Elisabeth understood immediately. She hit a button on the console and the balloon began to inflate. Hoskins didn't notice the cable coiling around him like a snake – not until it was too late.

With a sudden tug Hoskins was pulled into the sky, scattering papers and his telephone. The balloon ascended rapidly until it jerked to a halt, attached as it was to inflation tubes.

"Smart thinking, Imogen," said Elisabeth. "When help comes for us they'll be arresting him at the same time."

"Hey, Auntie," said Imogen. "You know how you said that the thief seemed to disappear into thin air?"

"Yes?"

"It looks like he really did do, after all."

If you enjoyed this book, look out for another Take 2 title:

the true story of the Hindenburg airship disaster,
which brought airship travel to a dramatic end.